Floodplain

by Isabel Gallego
illustrated by Holly Cooper

Chapters

Harcourt

Orlando   Boston   Dallas   Chicago   San Diego

Visit *The Learning Site!*

www.harcourtschool.com

The River Rises

It was the rainiest May in many years. David Autumnhorse stood on one of the levees that protected Saddlersville from the White River. He was awed by what he saw.

Normally, the White River lay far below. Now, muddy brown water swirled almost at his feet. Trees, boards, and other debris were carried along by the rushing stream.

Like many small towns, Saddlersville had been built on a floodplain. David knew the land was called a floodplain because it was likely to flood when the river rose.

"The river crested in Lyman this afternoon at 27 feet," David said to his sister, Marie. "If the rain doesn't let up, we're in real trouble."

"Well, it isn't seeping through the levees yet," Marie said. She had driven up that morning from Dallas, where she was a nurse. She gave the angry river another glance. "Come on. Let's find Tom Nathan and see how we can help."

Tom Nathan was the basketball coach at the high school. He was captain of the volunteers on this part of the levee. The whole basketball team was there helping out.

"We've got human chains going to the top of the levee," Tom said. "David, you fill these sacks with sand. Pass them along to the next person in the chain. Good to see you here, Marie. Are you up to tossing 40-pound sacks around?"

"Of course," Marie said, a little indignantly.

"Just making sure," said Tom. "Go join that chain over there."

More Water on the Way

"Tom, we just got a call from Finleysburg," said Mrs. Chastain. She ran a restaurant in town, but it was closed right now. Every person in town was needed to fight the rising river.

"The reservoirs there are about to overflow," Mrs. Chastain said. She had to shout to be heard above the thunder of the storm and the roar of the rushing river. "They'll have to open the gates and let some water out."

Tom frowned. "That's bad," he said.

Still, Tom knew that releasing water was the only way for Finleysburg to protect itself. If Finleysburg didn't let some water out of its reservoirs, the water would just keep rising. Soon, it would pour over the banks. Part or all of Finleysburg would be flooded.

"Okay, let's speed it up," Tom shouted. "We need to call all the radio stations in the upland towns. They aren't in any danger of flooding. Tell them to put out a call for volunteers. We're going to need all the help we can get down here in the floodplain."

David worked faster. He shoveled until he yearned for rest, and then he shoveled some more.

He thought of his parents' hardware store in town and his grandparents' farm a few miles away. He had helped his parents board up the store and pile sandbags around it that morning. His grandparents had left for higher ground, taking with them whatever their truck could hold.

David remembered the stories they had told him about the floods of earlier years.

Farming on the Floodplain

"Why would anyone farm on a floodplain if there are floods so often?" David had asked Grandpa Ed.

"Because a floodplain has the best soil for growing crops," his grandfather had said. He had pointed across his wheat field. "All this rich black earth was a gift of the river. The river gives, but it takes away, too."

"Our people have farmed along the White River for 2,000 years," his grandmother had added. "We dug reservoirs for the dry times, but we let the river flood the fields when it wanted to."

She gazed at her sturdy farmhouse and brightly painted barn. "You gain something when you build houses and barns that will last, but you lose something, too," she said. "In the old days, we'd just move the village to higher ground and wait it out."

"We're going to need another layer of bags here," Tom Nathan called. "The water is seeping through in places." Tom's voice brought David back to the present. He began to work even harder.

Tom threw a glance his way. "Autumnhorse, you look like you could use a break," he said.

"I'm okay," said David. His muscles were aching, but he felt proud that the coach had called him by his last name, as if David were one of his basketball players.

"Go on, take a break," Tom said. "There's food and lemonade in the high school gym."

The gym felt like a timeout zone. One long table held food for the levee workers. Other volunteers were rushing to keep it filled.

People were resting, eating sandwiches, and gulping down lemonade. They all looked as exhausted as David felt. Hardly anyone was talking. They didn't have the strength.

One corner had been fitted out as a first-aid center. David saw several people sitting on chairs nearby. One man was holding his wrist as if it hurt. A mother was hugging a crying child.

Dr. Espina was gently checking a teenager's arm. The doctor looked up and recognized David.

"David, did I hear that your sister is in town?" Dr. Espina asked. She looked as tired as everyone else. Her white jacket was smeared with mud from the people she was helping.

David nodded. "She's out on the levee, filling sacks of sand."

"See if the crew can spare her," Dr. Espina said. "I could use some more trained help here."

A Reason to Cheer

Then a cheer went up in the gym. It took David a moment to realize what had happened. The drumming and splashing sound outside had stopped. For the first time in four days and nights, it wasn't raining!

David hurried back outside. He splashed down the street toward the river. Two school buses turned the corner, spraying water. David saw them pull up across from the levee.

Men and women poured out, carrying tools. There were even a few boys and girls his age. They were volunteers from towns above the flood-plain who had come to help.

David gave Marie Dr. Espina's message. His sister hugged him before she left. "The sky is clearing up," she said. "If the rain doesn't start again, we have a good chance of avoiding a flood."

"More than a good chance," Tom Nathan said. "I think one more row of sandbags will be enough. The river has never risen higher than that here."

Then he turned to the new volunteers. "Welcome," he said, "and thanks for coming." He began sending them to stations along the levee. Adding another row of sandbags took a lot of muscle.

An hour later, Tom was walking the levee, encouraging the volunteers to keep working.

"Autumnhorse, are you still here?" Tom asked. "You've certainly been doing an adult's job. Why don't you go home and get some sleep?"

"I'll be okay," David said. He yearned for sleep, but there would be plenty of time to rest after the river had crested.

After all, his town needed him. Living in the floodplain, he would be needed again, too. There was a big price to pay for this rich farmland, but David was ready and willing to do his part.